EVANSTON PUBLIC LIBRARY

T5-CVE-315

3 1192 01437 6043

J Corbe.S
Corbett, Scott.
The home run trick.

DATE DUE

JUN 17 1986

INTERIM SITE

Books by Scott Corbett

The Trick Books
THE LEMONADE TRICK
THE MAILBOX TRICK
THE DISAPPEARING DOG TRICK
THE LIMERICK TRICK
THE BASEBALL TRICK
THE TURNABOUT TRICK
THE HAIRY HORROR TRICK
THE HATEFUL PLATEFUL TRICK
THE HOME RUN TRICK

What Makes It Work?
WHAT MAKES A CAR GO?
WHAT MAKES TV WORK?
WHAT MAKES A LIGHT GO ON?
WHAT MAKES A PLANE FLY?
WHAT MAKES A BOAT FLOAT?

Suspense Stories
MIDSHIPMAN CRUISE
TREE HOUSE ISLAND
DEAD MAN'S LIGHT
CUTLASS ISLAND
DANGER POINT: THE WRECK OF THE BIRKENHEAD
ONE BY SEA
COP'S KID
THE BASEBALL BARGAIN
THE MYSTERY MAN
THE CASE OF THE GONE GOOSE
THE CASE OF THE FUGITIVE FIREBUG
THE CASE OF THE TICKLISH TOOTH
THE RED ROOM RIDDLE
DEAD BEFORE DOCKING

THE HOME RUN TRICK

EVANSTON PUBLIC LIBRARY
CHILDREN'S DEPARTMENT
1703 ORRINGTON AVENUE
EVANSTON, ILLINOIS 60201

Bt 1274

THE
HOME RUN
TRICK

by Scott Corbett

illustrated by Paul Galdone

An Atlantic Monthly Press Book

LITTLE, BROWN AND COMPANY · Boston · Toronto

COPYRIGHT ©️ 1973 BY SCOTT CORBETT

ALL RIGHTS RESERVED. NO PART OF THIS BOOK MAY BE REPRODUCED
IN ANY FORM OR BY ANY ELECTRONIC OR MECHANICAL MEANS IN-
CLUDING INFORMATION STORAGE AND RETRIEVAL SYSTEMS WITHOUT
PERMISSION IN WRITING FROM THE PUBLISHER, EXCEPT BY A REVIEWER
WHO MAY QUOTE BRIEF PASSAGES IN A REVIEW.

Third Printing

T 03/73

Library of Congress Cataloging in Publication Data

Corbett, Scott.
   The home run trick.

   SUMMARY: The Panthers try desperately to convincingly lose a baseball game when they find out the
winners must play a girls' team.
   "An Atlantic Monthly Press book."
   [1. Baseball--Stories] I. Galdone, Paul,
illus. II. Title.
PZ7.C79938Ho   [Fic]   72-3478
ISBN 0-316-15693-0

ATLANTIC—LITTLE, BROWN BOOKS
ARE PUBLISHED BY
LITTLE, BROWN AND COMPANY
IN ASSOCIATION WITH
THE ATLANTIC MONTHLY PRESS

Published simultaneously in Canada
by Little, Brown & Company (Canada) Limited
PRINTED IN THE UNITED STATES OF AMERICA

To a baseball fan
Lydia Crowell Flandreau
in whose home
most of this story was written

THE HOME RUN TRICK

1

THE CLUBHOUSE in the vacant lot was filled to capacity. Three and two-quarters of the club's four members were inside.

Kerby Maxwell was there. Fenton Claypool was there. President Bumps Burton was there. And Waldo's forequarters were inside, while his hindquarters remained outside.

Waldo was sitting in the doorway because when the full membership was present there was not room enough for him to come all the way inside. He was a small dog, but not that small.

The talk was of baseball. Bumps, a big, chunky boy, was the catcher and best hitter on their neighborhood team, the Panthers. Fenton was their star southpaw pitcher. Kerby was a good, dependable second baseman who often held onto grounders out around the keystone sack — about as often as anyone else did, anyway.

"I'm gonna enjoy our game with the Wildcats tomorrow," growled Bumps, looking like a happy executioner. "With

Butterfingers Blatweiler and Moony Davis back in their lineup and those two ringers out of it, we ought to mop them up."

In their first game the Wildcats' pitcher and captain, Red Blake, had run in a couple of big kids from another neighborhood, and the Wildcats might even have won if they hadn't started a fight among themselves that made the umpire call the game.

"We'll clobber them," agreed Kerby. "Why, they couldn't even beat the Cougars last week. Of course, it was a tight game, they only lost by one run, but —"

"That's right, sixteen to fifteen, but still the Cougars won it, and they got eight hits off Red, and what's even more important —" and here Bumps paused to tap Kerby on the chest with one banana-like finger for emphasis — "what's more important, they played a great game in the field. That's where they beat the Wildcats; they beat them with their terrific defensive play. Only seven errors, that's all they made. Think *that* over!"

"It's a significant statistic," agreed Fenton, who could come up with tongue twisters like that when he felt like it. Fenton was a tall, thin boy who stood very straight and had a brilliant, scientific mind, and who was always very courteous and thoughtful and honorable — yet with all these faults, he was

4

still likable as far as his fellow club members were concerned.

And he was right about the statistic, of course. It was significant. Their teams played seven-inning games, and any team that averaged only one error per inning was definitely shaping up.

"I'll tell you the truth, I'm not even sure the Cougars aren't getting to be the team to beat," Bumps went on. "As soon as we've polished off the Wildcats tomorrow, we ought to line up another game with the Cougars."

"Good idea. They might make it interesting," said Kerby. The last time out they had crushed the Cougars 7–0, with the Panthers fielding four balls cleanly and Fenton accounting for the remaining outs by whiffing seventeen. But this time might be a different story.

Waldo yawned, displaying a healthy, attractive pink tongue. Waldo was not gripped by the conversation. He was only a so-so baseball fan. Cat-chasing was more his idea of an interesting athletic event. He had scarcely finished his yawn, however, when his floppy ears perked up and he backed outside. He stood looking in the direction of the street.

"What's with Waldo?" asked Bumps.

"Someone must be coming," said Kerby.

"It must be someone he knows," said Fenton. "He isn't barking."

A hard object beat an impatient tattoo against the side of their clubhouse, rattling the boards, and a high, testy voice summoned them forth.

"Look sharp, boys, I want to talk to you!"

They exchanged an astonished glance.

"It's Mr. Carmody!" said Kerby, and they moved so fast they very nearly forgot to let Bumps crawl outside first. Being club president, he considered that one of his privileges.

They were right about their visitor. The small old man with the brown felt hat perched on his head and the cane in his hand was Alfred J. Carmody in person, and Alfred J. Carmody owned the vacant lot in which their clubhouse stood. It was his cane that had thumped the boards. As usual, he seemed to employ the cane more for getting his way than for getting about.

With him was a small, plump man in sports clothes smoking a frazzled cigar that looked as if it might come apart at any moment. On each side of the cigar, however, his mouth was turned up in a smile, which was more than could be said for Alfred J. Carmody's.

Not that Mr. Carmody was all bad. The first time he showed up and found their clubhouse on his property, he ordered them to remove it by the following Saturday. Later on,

however, he had relented. He had allowed them to build a new clubhouse and stay put.

"Well! Hi, Mr. Carmody!" said Kerby nervously, while the other boys extended similar greetings. Kerby was nervous for fear the peppery old gentleman had changed his mind again. Their clubhouse was conveniently located an equal distance from their three homes. Kerby's was behind it, with Bumps's and Fenton's on either side of it.

"Afternoon, boys," said Mr. Carmody, and wasted no further time on pleasantries. "Now, listen, you belong to a ball team called the Panthers, don't you?"

"Why, yes, sir, we —"

"Thought so. Well, this is my nephew Charlie Fowler and I want you to do him a little favor."

"Oh. Why, sure. What?" said Kerby, relieved. If Mr. Carmody wanted a favor done, he would darn well get one done. They were in no position to refuse him anything. For that matter, very few local people were, because Mr. Carmody owned half the property in town.

"Thanks, Uncle Al," said Mr. Fowler. Still smiling around his frayed cigar, he took over. "Boys, how would your team like to receive one dozen brand-new official major league baseballs and one dozen brand-new top grade baseball bats?"

"Wow!" said Bumps.

"Gee!" said Kerby.

Fenton said nothing. He continued to listen intently.

"I'll tell you exactly what the setup is," Mr. Fowler went on genially. "I work for the Taylorville Sporting Goods people, promoting their baseball equipment. We have an exhibition baseball team of kids your age, and I go around this part of the country setting up games with local teams. It's all for fun, and you get the bats and balls win or lose." He chuckled, and added, "In fact, if you beat our team, I'll double the prize."

For the first time, Fenton spoke up.

"I don't suppose we've got much chance of doing that, have we, Mr. Fowler?" he asked in his polite, serious way. "I mean, I expect you have all the schoolboy champs on your team."

"Not at all! I'll guarantee you that's not the case," said Mr. Fowler. "Look, if we fielded a team like that to play against local teams, the games wouldn't be any fun. In fact, they would only make the local crowd mad — the folks that come to see the game — and we're not interested in making folks mad, we're interested in making them buy our sporting goods. So you may not win, but if you're any good at all it should be a close game. And if I didn't know you were good I wouldn't be here talking to you in the first place."

The boys exchanged surprised glances, and Bumps asked, "How did you know that?"

"When you hear, you're going to feel pretty proud," said Mr. Fowler. "A few minutes ago Uncle Al drove me over to your school field, because he knew a lot of your local sandlot teams practice there. Sure enough, we found some kids hitting fungoes who were just what I was looking for, so I talked to them about my proposition. I told them I wanted to line up the best team in town. Well, it turned out they had a team, but they said yours was the best team of all."

"What?" Kerby was amazed. "Who said that?"

"Manly young fellow with red hair. He said he hated to admit it, but you guys were number one. Now I call that pretty darn good sportsmanship."

"Why, that must have been Red Blake!" said Bumps, glowing with vanity. "Imagine a rat like Red talking that way! I guess there's some good in everybody if you wait long enough."

"Well, then, what do you say?" asked Mr. Fowler.

Bumps was big and strong, but he was far from being the fastest thinker in their club. An impartial survey would probably have rated him fourth. But he was the club president, and the Panthers' best slugger, and right now he was feeling chesty.

"Sure we'll play!" he cried. "And look out we don't beat your team!"

"That's the way to talk!" said Mr. Fowler. "It's a deal! Day after tomorrow at Forman Field."

"Wow! You mean, we're gonna play there?"

"That's right. Sunday at two o'clock, the Panthers versus the Taylorville Toms!"

"The Toms? Say, if that's short for Tomcats, that's great, because all our teams are named after cats, too."

"Oh, it's not short for Tomcats," said Mr. Fowler in a casual tone of voice, "it's short for Tomboys."

2

"YES, SIR, the Taylorville Tomboys — as slick an all-girl team as you'd want to see," Mr. Fowler went on smoothly, ignoring the fact that all three boys looked as if they had suddenly turned to stone. "The thing is, we feel more girls should be playing baseball just the same as boys, so that's why we got up this team, to show how well girls can play. They're a grand bunch of kids, I know you'll like them. They'll give you a good game, and everyone will have fun. Well, this is great, fellas! I'll drop around again tomorrow and fill you in on the rest of the details, after you've had a chance to get the good news around to the rest of your team about all those brand-new bats and balls you're going to get!"

Mr. Carmody gave their clubhouse a couple of sharp prods with his cane.

"Hmm. I hope this place is going to last you for a while longer," he snapped, shooting a warning glance their way. "I expect it will — provided you don't do something foolish, like disappointing my nephew."

12

Even though the boys had been struck dumb, at least one of their minds was still working, and with desperate speed. Somehow Fenton managed to summon up a smile.

"Don't worry, Mr. Carmody, we'll be there," he said. "Twelve brand-new bats and twelve brand-new balls — that's really something! Wait'll our guys hear about that! But . . ." Fenton seemed to be struggling with his conscience. "Well, I suppose we ought to just keep our mouths shut and grab the prize, but . . ."

Mr. Fowler had become attentive.

"But what?" he demanded, and his smile began to lose a little something around the edges. At the same time, Fenton's smile grew broader.

"Well, I'm afraid you've been taken in by a smooth talker, Mr. Fowler," he declared, and never had Fenton chosen his words more shrewdly. Mr. Fowler was instantly wary.

"How's that? What do you mean?" he asked, chewing alarmingly on his cigar.

Fenton chuckled.

"Well, I guess Red didn't want to play in your exhibition game on account of the girls or something — because he knows darn well his team is the best," said Fenton. "I don't suppose he told you about the only game we've played them, did he?"

13

"Well, no," Mr. Fowler admitted, frowning, "he didn't."

"He didn't tell you about how they were mopping us up and would have won by a dozen runs if the game hadn't been called?"

"No —"

Fenton shrugged.

"Well, you don't have to take my word for it, Mr. Fowler. Why don't you come to the field tomorrow and see for yourself? We're playing them again tomorrow afternoon at one o'clock." Again Fenton shrugged. "Of course, even though you'll see they're the best team, I guess maybe you'll still have to take us, because if Red Blake has decided he doesn't want the Wildcats to play in your game, you can't very well make them do it."

Once again Fenton had used his scientific mind, with its keen grasp of psychology, to splendid advantage. Sure enough, Mr. Carmody rose to the bait.

"Oh, is that so?" he snapped, waggling his cane around fiercely. "I've had some dealings with that Blake boy's father, and — Well, if I say the Wildcats are to play, they'll play! But I wish you'd decide *who* you want, Charlie, because I can't spend my whole day on this foolishness!"

Mr. Fowler was still brooding over the indignity of having been taken in by a smooth talker.

"Well, I think this young fella here has the right idea," he declared grimly. "The way to know what I'm getting is to see for myself. I want the best team in town, and no smart-alec kid like that redhead is going to stick me with second best!"

He nodded to Fenton.

"Okay, sonny, I'll be there tomorrow. I may be a little late, but I'll get there as soon as I can."

"Good!" said Fenton. But then his long, solemn face grew concerned. He took on the air of a person seized by a wistful hope. "One thing, though, Mr. Fowler — if we *do* beat the Wildcats this time, we still get to play in Forman Field, don't we?"

Mr. Fowler clapped him on the shoulder.

"You bet you do! Get out there and beat the Wildcats, and you're my team!"

"Great!" Fenton turned to Kerby and Bumps, who had been listening openmouthed, and put on a dazzling display of enthusiasm. "Hey, guys, we got to get the team together right away and start practicing!"

"See you tomorrow, fellas!" said Mr. Fowler, and he and his uncle walked away toward the street. And as they went, the boys could hear Mr. Carmody make a comment.

"Well, I'd forgotten how greedy boys can be. I guess they'll do *anything* for a dozen bats and balls."

16

"Sure they will. And besides that, they like the idea of playing in a big ball park like Forman Field," declared Mr. Fowler, chuckling comfortably. "That always gets 'em."

As soon as their visitors had gone a dozen steps, Fenton sagged like a spent runner. For once he crawled inside the clubhouse first, and for once Bumps was ready to overlook the breach of protocol. He followed Fenton almost humbly, and Kerby brought up the rear.

Fenton had given them his finest hour, and he was exhausted. Even Waldo seemed to realize he had been privileged to witness the performance of a lifetime.

"Wow! Am I glad to get in here outa sight!" cried Bumps. "One more minute and I would have bust wide open!"

"Fenton, you were tremendous! I never thought I'd see you be so — so —" Kerby sought for a word that would do justice to the occasion and finally found it, *"unscrupulous!"*

Fenton glared at him wildly.

"Listen, everybody has his limits, and I'm no different! If anybody thinks I'm going to stand on that pitcher's mound in Forman Field and pitch to a bunch of *girls* —"

"Who are probably terrific hitters —"

"And all the kids we know sitting in the stands watching —"

"Including every girl from our school —"

"And everybody laughing their heads off while those Tomboys clobber us —"

"It wouldn't matter whether they did or not!" snapped Fenton. "Don't you see? No matter what happened, we'd look terrible. If we beat them, we'd look like a bunch of bullies. And if they beat *us,* we'd never hear the end of it! We couldn't win, even if we won!"

"You said it! But anyway, Fenton, you sure took care of that Fowler creep! So now, all we gotta do is . . ."

That was as far as Bumps got. Slowly but surely, three deep wrinkles gathered on his forehead, and anxiety darkened his eyes. Obviously it had finally occurred to their president that they were not yet out of the woods.

"Hey! When we play the Wildcats tomorrow, sure as anything we'll beat 'em!"

Fenton all but clapped his hand over the presidential mouth.

"Bumps! Don't even *say* such things! Don't you see? Tomorrow we've got to play the greatest bad game of our entire history! Tomorrow we've got to go out there and *lose!*"

3

THE IDEA of playing to lose was so foreign to Bumps's way of thinking that it took a minute to sink in.

"You mean we'll try to strike out when we're batting, and fumble grounders and drop flies worse than usual?"

"Well, yes and no," said Fenton. "We've got to be careful how we go about it, for a lot of reasons. First of all, there's Mr. Caldwell."

Mr. Caldwell was a retired railroad man who lived across from the school grounds. He loved to umpire, and never missed one of their games.

"You're right about that," said Kerby. "If Mr. Caldwell ever thought we were trying to throw a game, he'd never umpire for us again."

"No, and he'd tell us off then and there, in front of everybody — including Mr. Fowler. And if Mr. Fowler thought we were trying to pull a fast one, *he'd* jump all over us and tell Mr. Carmody, and then we could kiss this place goodbye," said Fenton, patting the splintery wall of their beloved clubhouse. "And even that's not all we're up against. If we look too bad tomorrow, the Wildcats are going to get suspicious. Red Blake is nobody's fool, so we've got to be careful not to let him guess what we're doing."

For a moment there was silence. It was depressing to realize how dark and devious was the path that lay ahead of them.

"Well, then, how *are* we gonna work it, Fenton?"

"It won't be easy. We've got to look as if we're trying our hardest, but just not clicking. Take me. I'll have to look as if I'm having trouble with my stuff. I'll pitch a couple of bad innings, then tighten up and pitch a good one. We've got to pace it so that nobody will suspect anything. Above all, we've got to make sure they keep getting more runs than we do."

Bumps released a windy, unhappy sigh.

"I sure hate to let Red Blake and his bums think they can beat us!"

"Listen, forget that and think about when the game is over and Mr. Fowler steps up and says to Red, 'You're not fooling me with your talk about the Panthers being best! *You're* the team I want!' Can't you see Red's face when that happens?"

For the first time in quite a while, the clubhouse rang with laughter.

"Well, I guess you're right, Fenton. We've got to go

20

through with it," said Bumps. "So what say we start circulating around the neighborhood to tell the other guys —"

But Fenton interrupted him with a shake of the head, and a careworn expression etched itself deeply into his solemn face.

"That reminds me of one more problem we've got," he told them.

"Aw, come on! Ain't we got enough already?" protested Bumps. "What else is there?"

"There's the rest of the team, that's what," said Fenton. "Don't forget, we're the only ones with anything to lose. We stand to lose our clubhouse, but that's nothing to the rest of the guys. So what's to keep them from playing their best and then refusing to play the Taylorville Tomboys if we beat the Wildcats?"

Bumps had the answer to that one.

"Me!" he growled, and his beefy shoulders seemed to bulge against the clubhouse walls as he flexed his muscles. "I'll knock their heads together, one by one, if they start that kind of talk."

Kerby wanted to know how Bumps could knock one head together, but decided it was not the sort of question to ask him when he was worked up. Bumps might show him.

"Well, maybe that will do it, and if it will I'm all for it," said Fenton. The threat of having to pitch against a girls'

team had made him absolutely ruthless. "Still, that's kind of a negative approach. Maybe I can think of something before we have to tell them. But if you ask me, we shouldn't tell the other guys anything yet, anyway."

"Huh? Why not?"

"Well, if we do, someone might slip up and talk in the wrong place, and the Wildcats might get wind of what we're up to. This is one secret we've got to guard with our lives!"

Bumps thought this over, and began to nod.

"Fenton, you're right again. You take blabbermouths like Buddy Bedford and Stevie Rizzo, they'd let something slip for sure. Okay, we won't tell them anything till they get to the field. That way there won't be any slipup."

From a distance a high, squealy voice penetrated their inner sanctum.

"Bum-m-m-m-mps!"

"Aw, what does *she* want? Outa the way, Waldo," growled Bumps, and stuck his head out the door. They had all recognized the strident tones of his sister Althea.

"Whaddaya want, Althea?"

"Mom's got some jobs for you to do and she wants them done *now!*"

Bumps turned a murderous scowl back in the direction of his clubmates.

"Someday I'll wring her neck. You wait and see," he told them. "Nothing she likes better than passing along orders. Okay, meeting's adjourned, see you later —"

"Bum-m-m-m-mps!"

"Aw, shut up, Althea, I'm coming!"

Kerby started to follow their president outside, but found Fenton's hand on his arm, silently telling him to stay put. As soon as Bumps had gone, Waldo lost no time taking his place inside. They listened to their president's voice recede toward his house, exchanging insults with his sister all the way, and then Fenton spoke.

"I've got something to tell you I couldn't tell Bumps."

"What's that, Fenton?"

"Well, I want to make *doubly* sure the Wildcats beat us tomorrow. If only we can put together some more of that stuff Mrs. Graymalkin had us make the first time we played them . . ."

Kerby could scarcely believe his ears.

"What? But that stuff was supposed to help us win!"

"That's right."

"But you didn't approve of using something that would help us win. You didn't think it was fair."

"I know," said Fenton, tight-lipped, "but this is different. This time it's going to help the *Wildcats* win!"

"Oh!" Now Kerby understood, and for a moment he brightened up. "Hey, that's a great idea!"

But then his face fell.

"Wait a minute, Fenton. When we mixed the chemicals to make that stuff, we used up all there was of both of them. And when we got to the ball field you poured out the whole tube."

This was no news to Fenton.

"I know," he sighed.

"Then how can we make any more?"

"Well, I'm just hoping we didn't really use it all. You know how it is, when you drink a bottle of pop and think you've finished it, there's always a little left in the bottom of the bottle? I'm just hoping there's some left in the bottom of those tubes."

"Say!" Kerby perked up. "It's worth a look, all right. It doesn't take much of that stuff to do the job."

"Well . . . at least we can check."

"Sure! What have we got to lose?"

"Tomorrow's game, I hope!"

4

WHAT they were talking about was Kerby's chemistry set, which he had acquired in an unusual way.

Late one afternoon in a small public park near home he had encountered a strange-looking old lady standing beside a drinking fountain with the heel of her shoe caught in the drain at the bottom of the fountain.

She was dressed in a draggly black dress with a draggly black cape over it, and a large black hat with a long straggly feather drooping from it, and high-heeled shoes instead of the more sensible shoes you might expect such an old lady to wear.

Kerby helped her work her heel loose from the drain. She told him her name was Mrs. Graymalkin, and that because he had been so nice to her she wanted to give him a present. The present turned out to be an old chemistry set her own son Felix had played with when he was a little boy.

Since then Kerby had met her often in the park, and had

used the chemistry set several times. Whenever he did, the results were amazing, as for example at the time of their first game with the Wildcats. Thinking about it as they walked toward his house, Kerby hoped Fenton would be right, and that some of the two chemicals they used then would still be left in the tubes.

Pushing aside the loose board in the fence between the vacant lot and Kerby's backyard, they slipped through, ran to the back steps, and hurried into the house. No one was home, which suited them fine. Other than Kerby and Fenton, the only ones who knew about Mrs. Graymalkin and the chemistry set were Waldo and Kerby's little cousin Gay.

They crossed the kitchen and went down into the basement, where Kerby kept his chemistry set hidden in a large wooden chest. He had been given the chest years ago to keep his toys in. The set was concealed under a lot of wooden blocks he had used to build forts and castles with back in the days when he played with toy soldiers.

Kerby dug out the set and put it on his father's workbench. In the long wooden box were a row of tubes in one section and various glass beakers and eyedroppers in another. Inside the plain lid, in faded red and black lettering, were printed the words:

FEATS O' MAGIC CHEMISTRY SET
Instructive!   Entertaining!
Hours of Amusement!
Astonish Your Friends!
Make Extra Money Giving Demonstrations!

"Okay. Now then, do you remember. the tubes we used?" asked Fenton. "One had a label on it that read 'Flt' —"

"And the other was labeled 'Slp.' "

"Right. And I know we put them back after we mixed the stuff, so . . . Sure! Here's Flt —"

"And here's Slp!"

They examined the two tubes, holding them up to the light, and looked at each other with a wild hope. Fenton's pop bottle theory was correct.

"There *is* a little bit left in both of them!" said Kerby.

"Yes, but is there enough? Last time Mrs. Graymalkin said we'd need about a tablespoon of the stuff. I'll bet there isn't half a teaspoon left between the two of them."

Staring at each other, they considered their predicament. Then Kerby spoke.

"You know, if you ask me, after dinner tonight we ought to —"

"Just what I was thinking," said Fenton.

It was a meeting of the minds. Their course was clear.

"Yes, you may go over to the park for a while with Fenton," said Kerby's mother after dinner, "just so you're home before dark."

"Don't worry, Mom, we will be," said Kerby, and ran outside to meet his friend. Waldo came along, of course.

"Well, I hope she's taking her constitutional tonight," said Kerby as they hurried down the street. That was what Mrs. Graymalkin called the walk she took almost every night in the park, her constitutional.

"This should be about the right·time," said Fenton. As he had pointed out before, she never seemed to show up until it was getting on toward dusk and the trees were throwing deep shadows on the pathways in the park.

"I don't see Nostradamus anywhere," Kerby remarked as they crossed the street to the park. He was referring to her ancient sedan, which she called by that name.

"Maybe she parked him in a different place this time," said Fenton.

"Maybe she isn't here yet. I hope she shows up!"

As usual, the park was deserted at that hour. Except for a few squirrels who teased Waldo as he went by, they had the place to themselves when they ran down the slope toward the drinking fountain. A lawn sprinkler had been left on near the path by some forgetful park attendant, but they ran quickly through its fine spray without stopping.

They walked up and down the path. There was no sign of Mrs. Graymalkin. Despondent, they sat down on a bench. Waldo flopped down in front of them.

"Well, we'll just have to wait and see."

"That's all we can do."

Under the trees the daylight was growing dim and fuzzy. Perfect conditions for Mrs. Graymalkin — but where was she?

To pass the time and take his mind off their troubles, Kerby decided to needle Fenton a little about their strange friend. Being of a scientific turn of mind, Fenton had decided views about her. As for Kerby, he was not so sure.

"I wonder if Gay could be right?" he said slyly, referring to his little cousin. "She really believes Mrs. Graymalkin is a witch."

As always, Fenton was aroused.

"Well, she's wrong," he snapped. "There's no such thing. Listen, Kerby, where did you first meet Mrs. Graymalkin?"

"Over there by the drinking fountain."

"And what is it witches are supposed to be afraid of?"

"You mean water?"

"Yes! So if there *were* such a thing as a witch, she certainly wouldn't hang around a drinking fountain!"

"She wasn't hanging around it. She was trying to get away."

"Well, all the same —" began Fenton, and then nearly shot into the air off the bench as a creaky voice behind them said, "Why, good evening, boys!"

They turned to find Mrs. Graymalkin stepping onto the path.

"Dear me, did I startle you, Fenton?" she asked with a sly cackle as they sprang to their feet. "How nice to see you both, and dear little Waldo as well!"

Mrs. Graymalkin was wearing her summer-weight black dress and a black silk shawl. In keeping with the season she had even substituted a black straw hat for her usual wintry flipflopper, and its long black feather looked like something an ostrich might have shed in warm weather. Missing, however, was her customary snaggle-toothed smile. Instead she looked cross and ruffled.

"I declare, these park people are becoming more careless all the time!" she complained. "One of them left a sprinkler on, and I had to walk far, far around it to get here!"

5

THE BOYS shot a round-eyed glance at each other. Fenton cleared his throat.

"Well, that's too bad, Mrs. Graymalkin," he said in a slightly squeaky voice. "But we're glad you came."

"I'll say we are!" said Kerby. "We've got a problem."

"Oh, dear, oh, dear, oh, dear, not another one!" sighed Mrs. Graymalkin. "Whatever is it this time, boys?"

They told her about the dirty trick Red Blake had played on them. When they had finished, her sharp old eyes were twinkling amid their tangle of crow's-feet, and she disappointed the boys by sniggering heartlessly.

"A girls' team! My goodness gracious, I don't know anything about baseball, but I'd love to come and watch that game myself! But why did you want to see me?" she asked, suddenly severe. "I certainly hope you don't expect me to help you defeat a *girls'* team!"

"Don't worry about that, Mrs. Graymalkin!" cried Kerby. "We don't even want to play them!"

"We want to make sure we *won't* play them," added Fenton. He told her about their scheduled game with the Wildcats, and that Mr. Fowler would be on hand to see which was the best team.

"So we have to make sure the Wildcats beat us tomorrow," explained Kerby, "because if they don't, Mr. Fowler will pick our team to play the Taylorville Tomboys, and then we'll either have to play them or lose our clubhouse."

"Lackaday!" said Mrs. Graymalkin. "You do have a problem indeed. Well, I would enjoy watching you play the girls, but I suppose I really must help you in some way if I can."

"Well, I certainly hope you will," said Fenton earnestly. "I can't tell you what it would be like to pitch to a bunch of giggling girls —"

"Perhaps they won't giggle," said Mrs. Graymalkin. "Perhaps they will be grimly in earnest."

"That would be worse!"

"Mercy me! Well, now, tell me, what sort of help did you have in mind?"

Fenton told her about the tubes of Flt and Slp.

"Hmm. It was clever of you to think of that, Fenton, but I must agree with you, I am very much afraid the amount you say is left would not be effective. If you used it the same way as the last time, when you mixed it with the drinking water in their team's water bucket, it would simply not be sufficient. So let me see, let me see, let me see . . ."

And to "see," Mrs. Graymalkin closed her eyes tightly and laid a long, bony index finger alongside her long, bony nose. The boys had come to refer to that digit as her thinking finger, because she always placed it in the same position when she was thinking hard. And it seldom failed to get results.

The way her eyes popped open presently showed it had not fallen short on this occasion, either.

"Under the circumstances, I am afraid there is only one thing we can do," she announced. "Now listen carefully."

She did not have to make this suggestion twice. Fenton's cup-handle ears seemed to be quivering at attention as he strained forward, and Kerby was no less intent when she began her instructions.

"Pour the small amount of Slp into the Flt tube, thus mixing it with the equally small amount of Flt. Have you got that well in mind?"

"Slp into Flt," said Fenton tersely, and she continued.

"Next, add two drops of a third chemical, which you will find in the tube labeled —" she paused to take in a deep breath, then rattled it off — "Bluboraxophenoloxidalkalimentholacticalciumate. You won't have any trouble locating it, because it has such a long name. I usually call it Blub for short."

"I think we'll do that, too," declared Kerby.

"It might save you time," she conceded. "But now, a word of warning. This mixture cannot be used in their drinking water. That would be bad, very, very bad — and besides, it wouldn't do the trick."

"Then how shall we use it?"

"I'll come to that," said Mrs. Graymalkin. "Now, when you are ready to add the two drops of Bluboraxophenolox — of Blub, be sure to wear masks, and even then hold your breath as well. Add the two drops and then cork the tube as fast as you can, *quickly quickly quickly!* After all, you will be doing this in your house, and you wouldn't want your parents to observe you acting as though you had suddenly become outstanding athletes, now would you?"

"I'll say not!"

"Very well, then, take care you don't get a whiff of the mixture. Now, as to how you will use it. Tell me, is there a place where each team gathers during the game?"

"Sure, we both have benches on the sidelines."

"Excellent. And do you suppose you could think of some plausible excuse to run past behind their bench while they are sitting on it, Fenton?"

"I'll think of something."

"I'm sure you will. Well, now. The mixture in the tube will

form a vapor. When you uncork the tube, the vapor will be released. So what you must do is run past behind the Wildcats, holding the tube inconspicuously in your hand at your side, and uncork it as you pass by. Be sure to hold your breath and continue to run past as fast as you can. Oh, yes, one other thing. Don't use the mixture until you reach some crucial point in your game when it's really needed."

Why not, Mrs. Graymalkin?"

"Because this Blub-Slp-Flt mixture is very powerful, but not long lasting. So use it when it will count."

This brought an anxious question from Fenton.

"How long *will* it last?"

"Oh, five minutes, maybe ten, but no more."

"Oh. Well, that's not too bad," said Fenton. "In our games you can make a lot of runs in five minutes, let alone ten. Thanks, Mrs. Graymalkin, that's just what we need!"

"Splendid, splendid, splendid. I hope you have a very satisfying defeat tomorrow," she told them, but added with a cackle, "I still say, though, it might have been quite a treat to watch you play those dear little Tomboys!"

38

6

WHEN THEY HAD SAID good night to Mrs. Graymalkin and started home, the boys were feeling better. Better, yet far from carefree. Kerby mentioned one care they were not yet free of.

"The stuff sounds fine, but what's going to be your excuse for running past the Wildcats' bench in the middle of the game? When they're sitting on their bench, you're out on the mound pitching to them."

"I know. I'm working on that," said Fenton, and the wrinkles on his high forehead bore him out. "There's got to be a way."

"Well, I hope so. And another thing that worries me is, what are we going to do with the tube till we're ready to use it? It won't be like last time, when you poured out the stuff before the game even began. This time we've got to wait till after the game's started. How can you play ball with a glass tube in your pocket? Even if you pack it in a little box like last time, it's liable to get broken."

"I'm working on that, too," said Fenton. "Right now let's just take care of mixing the stuff together and getting it ready."

They ran up the terrace into Kerby's front yard and started around the side of the house. Ahead of them two squares of light glowed on the ground, light from the basement windows.

"Darn! Someone must be in the basement," said Kerby. They peered through the windows, and he groaned.

"Omigosh! Pop's working on his table!"

The cards seemed stacked against them. Tonight, of all nights, for his father to have one of his rare attacks of carpentry — it didn't seem fair!

Mr. Maxwell was one of those men who periodically get the urge to build something, and invariably decide on some difficult project beyond their modest capabilities. He was an amateur carpenter who might turn out a reasonably good pencil box or a small breadboard if he stuck to simple designs. But instead, he always attempted something fancy and complicated. When the creative urge seized him this time, he had decided to build a gateleg table.

The struggle had been going on for nearly a year. First he would work away like a beaver for a night or two, slaving at his workbench, uttering low curses from time to time which Mrs. Maxwell did her best to keep Kerby from hearing. Then

40

he would give up in despair and brood about his project for a month or so. Then one night he would suddenly decide to go down and give it another try. And so it went.

"Wouldn't he have to pick tonight?" complained Kerby. "What'll we do?"

"We'll just have to hope he gives up before we have to go to bed," said Fenton.

When they entered the kitchen, they found Kerby's mother putting away clean plates and glasses from the dishwasher. She pointed to the basement door and gave them a warning.

"Better not go down there. Your father's working on his table."

"I know. We saw him through the windows."

Mrs. Maxwell sighed a wifely sigh.

"How I rue the day I ever said I liked gateleg tables!"

Kerby was rueing it, too, and so was Fenton. Waldo looked up at Mrs. Maxwell sympathetically, and then applied himself to cleaning up a few scraps still left in his dish. Life had to go on, in spite of sorrows.

The boys helped Mrs. Maxwell put away the dishes and then she left the kitchen, after first reminding Kerby that bedtime was approaching. Once his mother was safely out of earshot, he mentioned a new cause for concern that had occurred to him.

42

"I just thought of something terrible!" he muttered in a low voice. "Come on outside!"

For greater safety they stepped out and sat on the back steps to talk.

"Fenton, we've got to mix that stuff tonight!" said Kerby. "You remember how it was last time, the stuff had to stand overnight!"

"Yes, I know, but Mrs. Graymalkin didn't say *this* mixture did. And if it did, she would have said so." Fenton tried hard to sound confident, but then he added, "I wish we'd thought to ask her, though, just to be sure."

"So do I!" After squirming uncertainly for a moment, Kerby stood up. "I'm going to go take another look and see how Pop's doing."

Kerby reached the window just in time to hear his father talking out loud to himself.

"The darn thing, anyway!" he was growling. "I'm going to get this leg right if it takes all night!"

All night! That meant he would still be at it long after they were in bed. When Fenton heard the news, he said, "Well, we'll just have to mix the stuff in the morning and hope it's all right."

And on this uncertain, worrisome note they parted for the night.

The Maxwells were finishing breakfast the next morning, and Kerby was wondering how soon Fenton would come over, when he received a new blow.

His father sat back from the table and put his napkin down with an air of determination. Mr. Maxwell's face looked rather drawn. There were definite circles under his eyes.

"Darn it, I could hardly get to sleep last night, thinking about that fool leg," he announced, "but I think I figured out what I've been doing wrong. I'm going down right now and take another crack at it."

Kerby very nearly let out a banshee wail that would have made his mother feel his pulse and take his temperature. He had forgotten it was Saturday! Saturday, and his father didn't have to go to the office!

7

SITTING IN THE CLUBHOUSE later that morning, where he and Kerby had gone to talk things over, Fenton slowly shook his head.

"This is terrible," he said. "And I've got everything else worked out, too! I did a lot of thinking last night, and I hoped we were all set. I figured out an excuse to run past the Wildcats' bench, and I figured out how I could carry the tube to the game. But now . . ."

From down in Kerby's basement the sound of sawing reached their ears like a mournful dirge. To pass the time while they hung around hoping something would happen to get Kerby's father out of there, they got their gloves and an old baseball and started throwing up pop flies for each other. Before long, however, Kerby managed to release a wild throw, and the ball came down on the garage roof. It rolled into the gutter, far out of reach, rattling dead leaves as it settled down like a squirrel in a nest.

"Aw, the heck with it," said Kerby gloomily. "Pop will get it later."

Mr. Maxwell had a strict rule against ladder-climbing. Once when he was a boy he had fallen off a ladder he was not supposed to climb on. The experience had left its mark on him, not physically but psychologically.

All at once the sound of the ball rattling those dead leaves sent a delayed thrill up Kerby's spine. His father had been talking for weeks about how he ought to climb up and clean out that gutter. . . .

A moment later the boys were inside and Kerby was calling down the basement stairs.

"Hey, Pop, we were throwing up pop flies and the ball landed on the garage and rolled into the gutter," he whined. "Can we use the ladder to —"

An impatient snort whistled up the stairway.

"Kerby, you know you're not to climb up on ladders!"

"Well, gee, Pop . . ."

This time a martyr's sigh answered his plea.

"Oh-h-h! . . . Okay, I'll come up and get it down for you. Bring the ladder out of the garage and put it in place, and I'll be up in a minute!"

When the craftsman appeared, the ladder was in place.

"Now, if you can't keep the ball off the garage roof, don't

throw any more pop flies, you hear me?" he said in a cranky voice as he mounted the ladder. "I'm very busy! Furthermore, I don't see any ball up here. . . . Oh, yes, here it is. Almost buried out of sight! Good Lord, these leaves are even worse than I thought! It's a wonder we haven't had some leaks —"

Mr. Maxwell glared at the leaves.

"Darn it, there's always something to drag a man away from . . . But I guess while I'm up here I might as well take a few minutes and get this mess cleaned out," he grumbled. "Kerby, bring me a couple of those bushel baskets from the back of the garage . . ."

The next few minutes were the most nerve-racking ones Kerby and Fenton had spent in a long time. But even so, as they rushed down the basement stairs, Fenton took the trouble to pant out an accolade.

"Kerby, that was sensational!" he cried. It was a simple tribute but a heartfelt one, and it filled Kerby with quiet pride.

Sensing drama, Waldo came along. He always liked to be where the action was. When they reached the toy chest, he sat down beside it and watched, fascinated.

Blocks flew aside. Out came the chemistry set. It was carried to the workbench and opened. Waldo moved over and got a good seat down front beside the workbench.

Kerby grabbed the Slp tube. Fenton grabbed the Flt tube. Kerby uncorked the Slp tube, and Fenton uncorked the Flt tube.

"Slp into Flt," muttered Fenton, and Kerby handed him the Slp. With a hand that trembled no more than an average aspen leaf, Fenton poured Slp into Flt. In the meantime, Kerby was locating the third tube.

"Here it is!"

The third tube was unmistakable. The name on its label was so long it ran all the way around the tube in a spiral. The last part of the name ended up under the first part. Uncorking it, Kerby handed the tube to Fenton.

"Careful, now. Two drops."

"Two drops," nodded Fenton, "and the minute they're in, jam in the cork. Oh, gosh, wait a minute — we're forgetting masks! Mrs. Graymalkin said to put on masks."

In a pile on a back corner of the workbench were several threadbare bandannas, to be used as rags. Quickly the boys each tied one around his face, over his nose.

"And hold your breath when I drop in the two drops," Fenton reminded Kerby.

Once again he picked up the Flt tube, which he had carefully braced in a corner of the box. Trembling though it was, his hand did not fail him. In went two drops of Blub, no more

and no less. And just as accurately, Kerby jammed home the cork.

Like surgeons removing their masks after a difficult operation, they pulled off their bandannas and grinned with relief. Fenton held up the tube.

"Look at that!"

It appeared to be full of a cloudy gray vapor.

"Well, I hope it does the trick," said Kerby.

They returned everything but the one precious tube to the box and restored the chemistry set to its hiding place under the blocks in his toy chest.

"We're all set!" said Fenton, and pulled out of his pocket another tube, larger and made of aluminum. He grinned at Kerby. "This is one of the tubes my father's cigars come in. Once in a while he likes to smoke a fancy cigar."

Producing some tissue paper, he wrapped it around the glass tube, slipped the one tube inside the other, and screwed on the aluminum cap.

"There!"

So preoccupied had they been with the critical job they were doing that not until then did the boys notice Waldo. Waldo's sense of smell was keener than theirs, and nobody had told *him* to hold his breath.

"Hey!" cried Kerby. "Would you look at Waldo!"

Waldo was walking up the stairs. There was nothing unusual about that, of course, except that this time he was walking up like a circus dog, on his hind legs.

They rushed after him in time to see him stop in the kitchen and do a very snappy back-flip somersault, landing on his feet.

Next he walked into the dining room on his front paws, then made a sensational leap over the dinner table without touching it. He followed this by springing up onto one of the chairs and balancing for a moment on the narrow ladder back as delicately as a cat on a fence.

Jumping down, he shook his head sharply, glanced up at the boys with a puzzled expression, and returned to the kitchen, where he had a long drink of water.

Kerby and Fenton stared at each other.

"He must have gotten a whiff of it," said Fenton.

"He sure must have. And if a whiff of it can do that for Waldo," said Kerby, "a good sniff of it ought to do wonders for the Wildcats!"

8

WHEN IT WAS TIME to go, the boys assembled at the clubhouse to walk over to the school field together. Bumps was carrying his catcher's equipment and a bat or two. Kerby and Fenton brought their gloves and bats and a couple of baseballs.

The will to win was strong in Bumps. He was still having trouble accepting the idea of throwing a game.

"Darn it, I feel like I could hit about six homers today!" he grumbled. "It's gonna be hard to hold them in."

"Don't worry, Bumps, you can hit a couple, just to make things look normal, once they've got a good lead," Fenton pointed out, and their star slugger felt better.

"Well, I can tell you one thing, those guys of ours better do as they're told and play losing ball, or I'll fix them! Maybe instead of knocking heads together I'll twist noses," he decided, and Kerby shuddered as he watched Bumps's cruel, banana-sized fingers bunch into nose-twisting formation. But at that very moment, Fenton had an inspiration.

"I've got it! I know how to handle them!" he announced, his eyes flashing with the zest of a brainstorm. "Instead of a negative approach, we've got to make a positive approach."

"How are you gonna do that?"

"Leave it to me and you'll see."

When they reached the field, most of the Panthers and Wildcats were already there, warming up. Among the Panthers were Rizzo, 3b, Stern, ss, and Bush, rf. While Kerby and his friends were approaching, they saw Stevie Rizzo drop a soft line drive, Tommy Stern let an easy grounder go between his legs, and Joey Bush miss a fly in the outfield.

"Now, that's the stuff we need," said Fenton. "I hope they save some of it for the game."

They were walking along the third base line. The Wildcats would be sitting on that side, while the Panthers would have the bench on the first base line. That much had already been settled by a toss of a coin several days ago.

Along with his other equipment, Fenton was carrying a jacket. Being the Panthers' pitcher, he naturally had to have a jacket to put on if he got on base, just like the big league pitchers. Of course, being the terrible hitter he was, Fenton seldom got on base. And today, needless to say, he intended to strike out even more than usual.

As they walked along the third base line past the left field

54

area, Fenton waited till Bumps was not looking and dropped his jacket on the grass outside the foul line. He winked at Kerby, who got the idea. *That* was how Fenton was going to give himself an excuse to run past the Wildcats' bench! When the time came, he would run up the third base line to get his jacket — as though he needed something from one of its pockets — and that would take him past the Wildcats' bench.

Red Blake was warming up on the sidelines with his catcher, Pinky Marshall's cousin Clyde. Red stopped throwing when he saw them coming, and greeted them with a smirk.

"Hi, guys. What's new?" he asked in a voice that dripped with innocence.

"You finally admitted we're the best team in town, that's what's new!" jeered Bumps. But Red only laughed in his face.

"Sure, wasn't that nice of me?"

Fenton spoke up.

"You won't think it's so funny when you hear what we're going to do tomorrow. We're going to play at Forman Field!" he said, sounding so proud Red blinked. After his first surprise, however, Red managed a sneer.

"Yeh, but who are you going to play? A girls' team!"

"So what? Do you know what we'll get for doing it? A dozen brand-new official major league baseballs and a dozen brand-new bats!"

"Well, lucky you!" said Red scornfully, and not a little astonished. "You sure must want them awful bad!"

"You're just sore because *you're* not getting them," said Fenton, and they walked on toward their own bench.

"I hope he hasn't said anything about this mess to our guys yet," muttered Kerby.

"Don't worry," said Fenton, "he was saving that for us. He never figured for a minute we'd agree to play a bunch of girls. Maybe he figured Mr. Carmody would threaten us, but he probably thought we'd give up our clubhouse before we'd play the Tomboys. Call our guys together, Bumps, and let me try my idea."

"Hey, Panthers! Over here!" bellowed Bumps, and the rest of their team came trotting in from the field. Meanwhile Red was busy getting his team together to tell them the news. Bumps gathered the Panthers into a tight huddle, and Fenton began to whisper his positive approach.

"Listen, guys, how would you like to see the Wildcats have to play a girls' team in front of everybody tomorrow at Forman Field?"

Their reaction was just what might have been expected. Delighted snickers, cheers, and laughter.

"Okay, here's what happened," said Fenton, and told them about the Taylorville Tomboys and Mr. Fowler. "Now, Mr.

56

Fowler is coming today to watch us, and the team that wins is going to be the one he wants. So all we've got to do is make sure the Wildcats win today, and they'll have to play a bunch of girls who will make them look silly in front of everybody!"

Fenton's approach was right on the button. It worked. A lot of excited whispering went on, and more snickering and chortling, and in no time the Panthers were all set. From his side of the diamond, Red Blake looked on with haughty disgust and gained a completely false impression of what was going on. Kerby strained his ears for Red's reaction, and heard him say to Eddie Mumford,

"My gosh, they're *happy* about it! What a bunch of sissies!"

He turned and called out to the rest of his team in a high falsetto voice.

"Well, come on, girls, here comes Mr. Caldwell, so let's powder our noses and get ready to play the mean old Panthers!"

Bumps straightened up and glared around at him.

"Aw, shut up, Red!"

"We're just using you pushovers for batting practice," yelled Fenton. "I'm glad you know who's the best team, because we're going to mop you up today."

His cocky remarks accomplished their purpose.

58

"Oh, is that so?" Red yelled back at him, his redhead temper flaring. "We'll see who's the best team!"

Mr. Caldwell was hurrying across the field, but he was not carrying his umpire's mask. At first Kerby thought that for some reason he was not going to umpire the game, but then he bustled toward them shouting his usual message.

"All right, boys, let's play ball, I haven't got all day! I ought to be home finishing my trim," he grumbled guiltily. Mr. Caldwell always had some chore he should have been finishing up at home, and he always came over and umpired instead. Last time it was shingling his roof. This time it was painting the trim on his house. But here he was, as usual.

"Where's your mask, Mr. Caldwell?" someone asked.

"Chin pad came loose and I haven't had time to fix it yet," he replied. "I'll stand behind the pitcher to umpire today. I can see the bases better that way, anyhow. Okay, Wildcats up first, same as last time, because you never finished that game. Play ball!"

It never occurred to any of them to argue with Mr. Caldwell, except to protest some of his close decisions, and that never did any good, anyway. The Panthers quickly took the field, and the Wildcats' lead-off man, Pinky Marshall, stepped into the batter's box. Just to make things look good, Bumps gave Fenton the signal for a fast ball, and Fenton burned one in right over the plate.

"Stee-rike!" yelled Mr. Caldwell, jerking up his right hand.

The big game had begun.

9

FENTON mowed the side down in the top of the first inning, striking out the first three batters, and the Wildcats took the field looking disgruntled.

"Got to make them good and mad," Fenton murmured when he and Kerby and Bumps were sitting side by side on the bench. "Okay, Kerby, start us off, but take it easy."

Kerby selected a bat from the pile alongside the bench.

"I wonder when Mr. Fowler will show up?"

"He said he'd be late. Don't worry about him, just get us an out."

Walking to the plate, Kerby stepped in and watched the first pitch go by. It was a sizzler, almost as good as Fenton's first pitch had been.

"Stee-rike!" yelled Mr. Caldwell.

Red looked as if he had his stuff today, which was good news indeed, under the circumstances. Kerby swung at the second pitch and nubbed a little grounder to Eddie Mumford at second.

It was a strange feeling to be racing to first and hoping Eddie *wouldn't* bobble the ball. Luckily he hung onto it and got it over to first in time for the putout. Kerby trotted back to the bench, where everybody tried to look disappointed in him.

Tommy Stern batted next and had no trouble striking out. Then Joey Bush hit a soft liner back to the pitcher, which was sure death, because Red was an all-around good ball player. Red squeezed it for the third out.

"Great inning!" muttered Fenton. "Now, this time let's go out there and get the Wildcats some runs!"

Being the Wildcats' cleanup man — batting fourth, that is — Red Blake was first up in the second inning. After wasting a couple of pitches, making it two and nothing, Fenton threw one that hung over the plate, and Red hit it out of sight. It was a home run all the way.

While Red circled the bases grinning broadly, Fenton made a great show of pacing around on the mound kicking dirt and acting disgusted with himself, and Kerby ran in from his position at second, pretending to talk to Fenton to settle him down.

Fenton appeared to be rattled by Red's homer, however, because he could not find the plate and walked the next man on four straight pitches. With the third batter, Bruce Carmichael, he managed better, making him hit on the ground to Kerby, but though he fielded the ball nicely, Kerby made a wild throw to the shortstop, missing the force at second, and the runners ended up on second and third. Fenton gave Kerby a dirty look.

"Come on, watch where you throw them!" he yelled.

"Well, I didn't do it on purpose!" Kerby yelled back, acting annoyed. He had to look away to keep from grinning.

Bumps called for an intentional walk on the next batter, Buzzy Dugan, since with first base open and the two weakest hitters coming up next it would have looked funny if he hadn't. For a pitcher like Fenton, Moony Davis and Butterfingers Blatweiler were normally a pair of sure strikeouts.

Bumps walked out to the mound and Kerby and Tommy Stern came from the infield to gather around Fenton. What they really wanted to do was try to decide what Fenton could possibly throw that Moony might hit. The only trouble was, Mr. Caldwell was standing right there where he could hear everything, so they had to say the same old things they would have said if they were trying to win.

"Okay, Fenton, strike him out!"

"You can do it!"

"Take care of him and Butterfingers, and then we'll worry about Pinky," said Bumps.

Fenton got the message. Bumps was right. Concede two outs, and hope Pinky Marshall would get hold of one and drive in three or four more runs.

"Okay, let's go, let's play ball!" ordered the umpire, and they all ran back to their positions. Fenton worked Moony to two and two, then put one past him while he stood looking at it. That brought Butterfingers Blatweiler to the plate.

Eager to get on with the game, Fenton burned two fast ones past Butterfingers. Then Bumps signaled a change-up, and Fenton sent one in at three-quarters speed. Butterfingers shut his eyes and swung.

Smack!

There is an old baseball adage that says, "Anybody standing up at the plate with a bat in his hands is dangerous." By the law of averages, even the worst hitter is going to connect with the ball once in a while. And Butterfingers did. The ball shot over Fenton's head and into center field, a clean hit.

An honest hit! It caught Buddy Bedford so much by surprise that it rolled past him. By the time he picked it up and threw it in, three runs were across and Butterfingers was sliding into third, trying to believe he wasn't dreaming.

This time Fenton really kicked some dirt around on the mound, and he wasn't acting. Sure, he wanted to see the Wildcats pile up plenty of runs, and all that, but at the same time he was a star southpaw pitcher, and it galled him to think he had given up a clean hit to Butterfingers Blatweiler, of all people. It was humiliating, no matter how good the cause.

Kerby ran in to the mound to calm him down.

"Take it easy, Fenton. It could happen to anyone."

"Aw, shut up!" said Fenton, which was most unusual, since ordinarily he was always so polite. Still, Kerby could understand, because when Fenton was pitching he was not his usual self. He was the way a good pitcher ought to be: mean!

Bumps had also come out to talk to Fenton. He walked him halfway back toward the plate, so that Mr. Caldwell couldn't hear what they said.

"Come on, now, Fenton, feed Pinky a good one and let's see if we can't bring Butterfingers home, too," he urged. But he was not reckoning with a star pitcher's vanity.

"Nuts!" snapped Fenton. And he went back to the mound and whiffed Pinky Marshall and Eddie Mumford for the second time in a row.

By then he was feeling better. When he walked in to the bench, he said, "Sorry, but I had to do that. Don't worry, four runs is enough for one inning. We'll give them plenty more later."

And he mollified Bumps by adding, "Go ahead and hit a homer this time. We can afford it."

Bumps marched happily to the plate and hit Red's third pitch into a gulley at the far edge of the field, making the score 4 to 1. Then Stevie Rizzo hit a straightaway fly to the Wildcats' best outfielder, Buzzy Dugan in center, and Buzzy caught it. The next two batters fanned.

In the top of the third Fenton grooved one for Pinky's big cousin Clyde that Clyde hit to right center for a double, and grooved another one for Red Blake that gave Red another homer and made it 6 to 1.

"I like that junk you're throwing today, Fenton!" yelled Red as he circled the bases. "Keep it up!"

Fenton only scowled at him, kicked some dirt around, and fanned another batter. Next Bruce Carmichael hit a grounder Kerby's way and this time Kerby was able to bobble it convincingly and let Bruce get to first.

"Come on, Kerby, that's the second time in a row you've let him get on!" yelled Fenton.

"Aw, shut up and pitch, will ya?" snarled Kerby.

Buzzy Dugan lifted one to right field that Joey Bush dropped with the greatest of ease, and runners were on first and third. Unfortunately, Moony Davis was up next. Fenton fed him soft stuff, but Moony still managed to whiff. That brought Butterfingers to the plate with two outs.

Kerby snickered into his glove and got ready to watch what would happen next, because he knew Fenton and Bumps had set up a plan of action for what to do if they had a man on third with two outs and a weak batter up. Fenton would throw one wide of the plate and Bumps would let it go off his mitt and roll past him. That way, another run would come across.

Fenton wound up and threw a pitch so wide of the plate that no batter in his right mind would have swung at it — except Butterfingers Blatweiler. Butterfingers lunged at it wildly, got the end of his bat on it, and dumped a soft liner over the first baseman's head down the right field line for another triple that brought in two more runs.

Fenton's face was red as a beet, but Butterfingers was delirious with joy. He was having himself a day. The Wildcats had eight runs, and he had driven in five of them himself!

Fenton was so mad he fanned Pinky Marshall for the third time in a row to end the inning.

"Eight to one! Wow, that's great!" Kerby said to him in a low voice as they left the field, but Fenton refused to rejoice with him.

"Two triples back-to-back to Butterfingers Blatweiler!" he snarled. "I'm not sure *anything* is worth that!"

In the bottom of the third, Buddy Bedford smacked a grounder that went through Bruce Carmichael's legs at shortstop. That brought up the weakest hitter on anybody's team, Fenton Claypool. Red Blake turned around and motioned to his team.

"Okay, sit down, everybody. Here comes Fenton!"

Like many weak hitters, Fenton usually tried to kill the ball. His ferocious swings made a breeze that nearly blew the caps off the outfielders, but seldom troubled the ball any as it traveled past into the catcher's mitt.

This did not prevent Fenton from taking himself seriously every time he stepped into the batter's box. On the present occasion it did not prevent him from deciding he should be extra careful not to get a hit. When Red threw him a lazy curve on his first pitch, wanting to play with him and make him look bad, Fenton took an easy swing at it and actually fouled it back.

Now it was Red's vanity that was injured. To have a hitter like Fenton hit a foul ball off him was like having anyone else smack a homer. He hitched up his belt and got ready to blow a couple past Fenton for his usual strikeout.

"Kill it, Fenton!" yelled Bumps, hoping to get him back on the strikeout trail, and to Kerby he said, "What does that nut think he's doing? If he keeps swinging like that, he's liable to hit one!"

On his second pitch, Red reared back and burned one in hard. Again Fenton took a nice smooth swing.

Clunk!

70

His swing was late, but not quite late enough. He got a piece of the ball and hit it toward left field.

Buddy Bedford, the man on first, took off the minute he saw where the ball was going. He could not have done anything else without everyone thinking he was crazy, because the Panthers' left fielder was Butterfingers Blatweiler, which meant that any ball hit to left field was sure to be a loose ball.

Butterfingers actually got his glove on the ball, but as usual it squirted through his hands and rolled away past him. By the time he picked it up and pegged it over Bruce Carmichael's head on his throw-in, Fenton was all the way around the bases and coming across home plate, with Buddy scoring ahead of him.

Fenton ran back to the bench beaming, while the team did a lot of phony cheering and bawled him out in low voices.

"What's the matter with you, doing a thing like that?"

"I'm sorry. I'm only smiling to make it look good," Fenton claimed, but they knew better. Fenton could not help getting excited any time he actually hit a baseball.

"Now it's only eight to three, and with the top of our batting order coming up!" Bumps pointed out. "If anyone gets on base, *I'll* come up! Then what am I supposed to do — *strike out?*"

Bumps, too, had his limits.

"Well, let's try to get out of the inning without any more damage," said Fenton. "Go ahead, Kerby, you're up. Get us another out!"

10

THE STRAIN of trying to lose was beginning to tell on everybody. Kerby stalked up to the plate in a sour mood, thinking, "Why do I have to do all the dirty work?"

It would have been nice if the Wildcats still had that big 8–1 lead and he could have tried for a hit, just for the fun of it. But Kerby was a team player, so he was ready to strike out if he could. He swung hard under Red's first pitch and missed it a mile.

"Stee-rike!"

Then Red started playing around again, trying for fancy pitches, and threw a high wide one, and one into the dirt, and one Kerby had to duck back from. Three and one.

Kerby was in serious danger of walking!

He made up his mind to swing at anything. Tensely he waited for Red's next pitch.

Down it came, heading for the center of the plate. Kerby decided he could take it for a called strike, rather than swing and risk hitting it, so he kept his bat on his shoulder — and at the last instant the pitch broke wildly on the outside.

"Ball four!" yelled Mr. Caldwell. "Take a walk!"

Feeling foolish, Kerby shot an embarrassed glance at the Panther bench as he trotted to first. His teammates were sending up a hollow cheer, but he could see that Bumps was fuming. Now, unless someone managed by some miracle to hit into a double play, an almost unheard-of event in their games, Bumps would have to come to the plate, and with at least one man on base.

But then, as Tommy Stern stepped in to bat, Kerby got an idea. Maybe he could save the situation and make himself look good by getting picked off first!

He danced off the bag and saw Red watching him out of the corner of his eye as he came down from his stretch. Kerby widened his lead recklessly.

Red whirled and threw. His throw was right on the mark to Pinky Marshall. They had Kerby by a couple of yards as he dove for the bag.

And what did Pinky do? He let the throw go through him, and Kerby had no choice but to jump up and take second while Pinky was running down the ball.

Now the chance for a double play was even less. Forcing a grin, pretending to be pleased with himself, Kerby took a

74

big lead off second and prayed for a liner to the shortstop, who could then double him off at second.

But once again Tommy Stern struck out. Then Joey Bush hit an easy one to Eddie Mumford at second. Eddie let it run up his arm like a trained mouse, and Joey was safe at first. And of course Kerby had to go to third on the play.

Two on, only one out, and Bumps up! A great situation in any other game, but in this one — terrible!

It was the worst moment of Bumps's baseball career. What was he to do? Was he supposed to stand up there and let Red Blake — Red Blake! — strike him out, just as if he were any old batter?

On the other hand, if he hit anything at all, it might go a country mile, and three more runs would come across!

Gritting his teeth, Bumps let Red's first pitch go by for a called strike. Red then tried to keep his stuff low and on the corners, and missed a couple of times to make it two and one. His next curve broke across the plate and again Bumps let it go by, but from his vantage point at third Kerby could see what a strain it was putting on their star slugger.

Perhaps if Red had caught a corner one more time with a fancy pitch, Bumps might have let it go by for a third strike. But instead Red got cocky and tried to sneak a fast ball past him.

This was too much for Bumps.

Smack!

The ball went straight for the only player on the Wildcats' team who could have got his glove up in time to catch such a hard smash. Red Blake. It was self-defense as much as anything. Behind him Mr. Caldwell nearly hit the dirt getting out of the line of fire. But Red held onto it and rifled the ball to Schultz at third, and Kerby was doubled off to end the inning.

The great Bumps Burton had hit into a double play!

Kerby was almost afraid to run back to the bench. He would have liked to go straight out to his position, but he had to get his glove.

When he approached the bench, Bumps was putting on his shin guards. He glowered up at Kerby, and Kerby could see that the banana fingers were ripe for action.

"Kerby Maxwell, if you weren't my friend I'd give your nose a twist that would leave you breathing upside down!"

"But gee, Bumps, you saved the day!"

"Huh!"

In the top of the fourth Eddie Mumford led off by hitting a little foul ball about ten feet in the air and straight up.

Bumps could hardly have dropped it if he had tried — and Bumps was not about to look bad twice in a row.

While Eddie was at bat, a skinny little kid came running down the slope from Bergmeyer Avenue and joined the Wildcats on their bench. He did a lot of talking to Red, and Red seemed to be paying close attention.

"Who's that, their new manager?" quipped Kerby as he came in and tossed the ball to Fenton after it had been thrown around the infield following Eddie's foul-out.

"I don't know, but I'd like to find out," said Fenton. "I don't like the way Red is looking."

"You think he looks meaner than usual?"

"Yes."

Clyde Marshall stepped in and hit Fenton's second pitch to center field, a long fly that looked good for a home run. Buddy Bedford made a great try for it. Too great, in fact, because when he reached up the ball was there, smack in the center of his glove. And having made a tremendous catch, Buddy couldn't quite bear to let go of it.

Now Red Blake was up again. He came to the plate swinging his bat fiercely, but then stepped in and let a couple of good pitches go by. For his third pitch Fenton really grooved one, right where Red could powder it. Red swung hard — and missed!

"Strike three! You're out!"

Red threw his bat aside disgustedly and took the ball Bumps tossed to him, and the teams changed places.

When he joined Kerby on their bench, Fenton was looking concerned.

"How could Red miss that last pitch?" he asked wonderingly. "Either he's slipping, or . . . Hmm!"

Stevie Rizzo led off in the bottom of the fourth with a little bouncer back to the mound. It was the kind of tapper Red could have handled in his sleep. But this time his foot seemed to slip, and he messed it up. Stevie was safe at first.

And by now Fenton's naturally long face was outdoing itself.

"Hmm!" he muttered once again, and a more worried mutter had seldom been uttered.

Pat Flanagan fanned, but when he came back to the bench he looked wrung out.

"I don't know how I managed to miss those pitches!" he reported. "Red's stuff was coming up to the plate like balloons! Nothing on it at all!"

Bumps was staring hard at the Wildcats' bench. Suddenly he clapped a meaty hand to his forehead.

"Crying out loud, I know who that little kid is! That's Splinter MacRae!"

Bumps was shamefaced and furious as he turned to Fenton.

"Last night Joey Bush came over and I told him what was up. I *had* to talk to somebody! And I made him promise not to say anything to any of the other guys, and he didn't — did you, Joey?"

"No!" said Joey.

"But my sister Althea must have heard us talking," Bumps went on, "and Nancy MacRae is her best friend, and I know she saw Nancy this morning. I'll bet she told her what she heard us talking about, and Nancy likes Red Blake — and Splinter is Nancy's kid brother!"

There was no question about it. Splinter had spilled the beans. Red and the Wildcats knew everything now. They knew what was going on, and they were out to lose!

Poor Bumps was nearly frothing at the mouth.

"I'll kill Althea! I'll kill her dead! So help me, I'll wring her neck like a washrag!"

Meanwhile Bingo Klotz was at the plate. The Panthers watched helplessly while Red appeared to have a wild streak, throwing the ball all over the place. He walked Bingo on four straight pitches.

Now there were men on first and second. Bumps turned to Buddy Bedford, the next batter.

"Do something, do anything, but don't get on base! Make

80

up for that darn ball you caught that should have been a homer for Clyde Marshall!"

Buddy batted left-handed. The first pitch was way outside. Jumping sideways behind the plate, Clyde caught it and got off a quick throw to first, which looked logical, because Bingo Klotz had taken a big lead off first and was standing flat-footed. He would have been an easy out; except that Clyde's throw went clear over Pinky's head into right field. Both base runners had to start running, and by the time Moony Davis finally got hold of the ball and threw it in, both runners had crossed the plate, and the score was 8 to 5.

This time it was Red Blake who was stamping around out on the mound and yelling at his fielders, but it was all an act, and the Panthers knew it was an act, and Red knew they knew it. Everybody on the field knew it but Mr. Caldwell, who was used to their errors and did not suspect anything.

After he had settled down, Red began to pitch to Buddy again. His second pitch was also way outside, but Buddy lunged at it and caught it on the end of his bat. The ball sailed straight to Schultz at third, and Schultz caught it before he stopped to think what he was doing.

The look Red gave his third baseman as Schultz tossed him the ball was as black as a look can get. Because now there were two outs and Fenton Claypool was up, and Red would look like a fool if he did anything but put them squarely over the plate for Fenton.

"For Pete's sake, Fenton, bat normal. Strike out!" hissed Bumps, as Fenton picked up a bat. "Get out there and try to kill the ball, so you'll miss it!"

"Don't worry," said Fenton, "I've learned my lesson!"

Pale-faced and determined, he strode to the plate and stood swishing his bat back and forth in a pathetic imitation of a .300 hitter. Red went into his stretch, came down, and threw.

Swish!

"Stee-rike!"

Again Red grooved one.

Swish!

"Two!"

The Panther bench exchanged furtive glances of joy. Fenton was swinging like the old Fenton, and there was nothing Red could do about it. No matter what he threw, Fenton could miss it, and Mr. Caldwell would never suspect anything funny was going on, because he was used to Fenton's missing everything.

Nobody was happier than Kerby to have old Fenton up there striking out to end the inning. Because otherwise, being the lead-off man, Kerby would have to bat next, and the last

thing he wanted to do was get up there with a man on base, now that Red knew what was going on.

Red grooved a third one.

Swish!

"Strike three! You're —"

But what was this? Catcher Clyde Marshall had dropped the ball! It was rolling away from him. Fenton had no choice but to run to first.

Kerby was horrified, and Bumps was humiliated.

"Why didn't *I* think of that one?" he groaned.

When the catcher drops a third strike, he must either tag the batter or throw him out before he reaches first. Dropping a third strike and letting it get away from him was a perfect way for the catcher to put an opposing player on base!

Meanwhile Kerby was suffering the tortures of the damned, a group he was beginning to feel he belonged to.

"Why me again?" he was wondering bitterly. "Why do I always have to be the one?"

Because now he was at bat, and how could he possibly get that third out against a pitcher who was determined to give the Panthers a bunch of runs?

11

NOBODY on the Panther bench said anything as Kerby picked up a bat. They just looked at him, which was worse.

What could he do? How could he possibly outwit Red Blake and get that third out?

Kerby stepped into the batter's box and watched Red's first pitch go by, low and on the outside.

"Ball one!"

Red's second pitch came over the plate looking the way Pat Flanagan had said, like a balloon. Kerby could have hit it anywhere, which was exactly what Red was tempting him to do. And as it floated up, Kerby had a flash of inspiration.

He bunted the pitch down the first base line and took off for first like a hare. He had never run faster in his life. Out of the corner of his eye as he shot past the Panthers' bench he could see a row of mouths hanging open and seven pairs of round eyes staring in horror. Because the bunt was a beauty, and even though Red made a great show of jumping off the mound to field it, anyone could see that Kerby was going to beat it out. Red picked it up cleanly and threw to first with the comfortable knowledge that his throw would be too late to beat Kerby.

With his usual enthusiasm, Mr. Caldwell had run over to be right on top of the play in true umpire style. By the time Pinky Marshall took Red's throw, Kerby had already shot past him. Foot on the bag, Pinky waited complacently for Mr. Caldwell's cry of "Safe!"

"Out!" cried the umpire.

Pinky was too astounded to keep still, as he would have in a normal game.

"What? Why, he beat the throw a mile!"

"Yes," said Mr. Caldwell, proud of his eagle eye, "but he missed the bag."

Kerby howled and leaped into the air waving his arms.

"What?" he cried. "I was safe!"

"You were not. You didn't touch first, so you're out, and don't give me any lip!" said Mr. Caldwell in the pontifical tone that is the trademark of any good umpire. Still grousing, Kerby stalked back to the Panthers' bench, a secret hero, while the Wildcats left the field gnashing their teeth.

The fifth inning was a battle of wits the like of which had never before been seen on the school diamond, and might never be equaled again.

Both sides tried every trick they could think of to make the other side score, and yet they had to be careful because of Mr. Caldwell. In the top of the fifth the Wildcats were unable to avoid scoring two more runs, making it 10 to 5. In the bottom of the fifth, Bumps tried to hold up on a good pitch, but his checked swing still dumped a double into right field that scored two runs, making it 10 to 7. After that the Panthers filled the bases, and before the third out finally came they had scored twice more, making it 10 to 9. And in the top of the sixth the Panthers were only able to force the Wildcats to score twice, which made it 12 to 9.

Kerby was first up in the bottom of the sixth, and managed to strike out this time in spite of everything Red could do. When he returned to the bench Fenton congratulated him, and then dropped his voice for a few private words.

"Well, now's the time, Kerby. As soon as we finish batting and the Wildcats come in to their bench, I'm going to get my jacket."

"Good! But I wish Mr. Fowler would come!"

"So do I. But no matter when he shows up, the more runs they make in the last inning, the better for us."

At the plate, Tommy Stern lifted a pop fly to short that Bruce Carmichael dropped. But then Joey Bush hit a beautiful little easy grounder to first that all but died at Pinky's feet.

87

There was nothing he could do but pick it up and step on the bag for the second out.

The only trouble was, now Bumps was up again.

As Bumps stood up to choose a bat, Kerby noticed two figures in the distance, walking toward the diamond.

"Hey! Here come Mr. Fowler and Mr. Carmody!"

"Great! Bumps, they're coming!" said Fenton, and immediately put this new development to good use. "Listen, Bumps, just this once you've got to strike out! Because if Mr. Fowler sees how great a batter you are, he might want us to play the girls anyway!"

Bumps scowled, and struggled with himself for a moment, but then he said, "I guess you're right. I guess I got to do it for the team."

"That's the spirit!"

Bumps went to the plate and let a couple of good ones go by. Red followed them with a fat pitch he was sure Bumps would not be able to resist. He was stunned to see Bumps swing at it and miss for strike three. The inning was over.

"Now!" said Fenton, and stood up. Kerby saw that he had sneaked the glass tube out of the aluminum tube while everyone else was busy watching the game. He had it clutched in his hand, all ready. Bumps had hardly finished his swing be-

fore Fenton started trotting down the first base line to go around behind home plate.

But as Bumps finished his swing he dropped his bat, and it came down squarely on the toes of the Wildcat catcher.

"Ow!" yelled Clyde, hopping around. "You big bum, you did that on purpose!"

"I did not!"

All the Wildcats came running in furiously except Butterfingers, who fell over his own feet and skinned his knee. And all the Panthers rushed off the bench except Kerby, who was too busy watching Fenton to worry about a hassle at home plate.

If someone had told Kerby he was having a nightmare, he would have believed it. He had that same helpless feeling as he saw Fenton surrounded and caught in the middle of the mob of arguing players. Spellbound, he watched someone bump Fenton's elbow. He saw the flash of the glass tube as it shot out of Fenton's hand and fell to the ground under all those milling feet. He could have sworn he even heard the crackle of glass as it was trampled on.

A swirl of dust seemed to envelop the players for an instant. It was a bit more grayish than ordinary dust, but nobody would have noticed who didn't know what Kerby knew.

Mr. Caldwell came halfway to the plate to restore order.

"All right, break it up! I had to call your last game because of a fight, but we're not going to have *that* again! Play ball!"

The squabbling stopped. A strange eagerness to play seemed to have come over the players.

"Okay, gang, forget it! We'll show them!" yelled Red.

"Take the field, guys!" yelled Bumps. "We'll slaughter them!"

Moving like big leaguers, the Panthers hurried out to their positions. Stepping like thoroughbreds, the Wildcats went to their bench and got ready to bat. Kerby tottered out to second base dreading to see what would happen next.

Except for Kerby and Butterfingers, who had been nursing his knee out in left field and now came limping in, every player on both teams had had a good sniff of the stuff in the tube. Out on the mound, Fenton was throwing in his warm-up pitches to Bumps, and they were something to see. Tommy and Stevie and Bingo were zipping the ball around the infield like pint-sized Baltimore Orioles. Tommy shot a throw to Kerby that nearly took him off his feet, and when Kerby threw the ball on to Bingo at first Bingo yelled, "Put some steam on it!"

Mr. Fowler and Mr. Carmody were close enough now for

Mr. Fowler to wave and call, "Hi, boys, how's it going?"

"Twelve to nine in favor of the Wildcats," croaked Kerby, "and we're just starting the last inning."

"Oh?" Mr. Fowler's eyes flicked around curiously. "Well, let's see you do your stuff."

"Yes, and make it snappy," said Mr. Carmody, settling himself on the Panthers' empty bench with his cane planted in front of him. "I haven't got all day!"

Kerby nodded and smiled wanly. Glancing around, he saw that the other players on both teams were taking little or no notice of the visitors. They were concentrating on playing ball. Kerby set himself at his position and wished he were far, far away, maybe home in bed, or even under it. Never had he felt more helpless and alone.

Anything could happen now!

12

PINKY MARSHALL stepped up to the plate, and the last inning was under way.

Fenton blazed one past the batter that made Mr. Caldwell's voice quiver with a connoisseur's delight as he yelled, "Stee-rike!"

Fenton's second pitch was just as good, and yet Pinky got his bat on it and ripped a clothesline drive into left field. Any other time it would have been good for two or three bases, but Pat Flanagan made a brilliant cutoff and rifled the ball in to second to hold Pinky to a single.

Eddie Mumford worked the count to three and two and then powdered a ball to Joey Bush in right field. It was over his head and looked like a sure home run, but Joey raced back with the crack of the bat and made a one-handed catch of it over his shoulder.

All the Panthers cheered except one, who groaned.

"Come on, hit one to me!" muttered Kerby, glaring at the next batter. "Give me a chance to let one go through!"

The batter, Clyde Marshall, did even better than that. He cracked a single over Kerby's head that sent Pinky to third. Now things were looking up. Men on first and third with one out, and Red Blake the batter! Now the Wildcats would get some runs for sure!

Red came to the plate looking like Superman. He hit Fenton's first pitch on the nose, belting a smoking grounder down the third base line just inside the bag. But who was this Superdooperman who flashed to his right and backhanded it? It was Stevie Rizzo! Kerby watched openmouthed as Stevie threw to Tommy Stern at second and Tommy ripped it over to Bingo Klotz at first. Mr. Caldwell's thumb jerked skyward.

"Out! Double play!" he yelled in a voice that cracked with excitement.

A double play around the Horn, as they say, third to second to first! Kerby had never before seen one in any of their games. And that made three outs. He left the field like a sleepwalker as the rest of the Panthers raced in past him, eager to get to bat.

Kerby could not even bring himself to glance at Mr. Fowler and Mr. Carmody as they moved over to the now empty Wildcat bench, because he didn't want to think about what Mr. Fowler would say when the Panthers won. How could they fail to win now? Even a fired-up Red Blake would never be able to hold these guys. The Wildcats had only a slim three-run lead. If the Panthers busted loose and made four runs it was all over.

But then, when Red Blake started pitching to Stevie Rizzo, Kerby began to hope again. Because Red seemed overpowering. His pitches were so fast the ball looked pear-shaped. Stevie went down swinging on three straight pitches.

Next, Pat Flanagan hit a wicked low line drive, but Eddie Mumford made a circus catch of it, diving sideways and spearing it with both feet off the ground.

Two outs!

But then Bingo Klotz hit one that nobody could get a glove on and made it to first. And Buddy Bedford, after fouling off a dozen terrific pitches, finally worked Red for a walk.

Fenton Claypool was up.

"Go up there and kill it, Fenton!" Kerby urged in a low voice.

Fenton gave him an affronted look.

"Don't be silly! If I try to kill it, I might strike out — and I intend to get a hit!" he said, and marched away to the plate.

It was plain to see that Fenton had gotten a king-size sniff of the stuff!

Sure enough, he hit the ball sharply between second and third. Ranging over unbelievably, Bruce Carmichael got his glove on it and knocked it down, and by doing so was able to hold Bingo at third and keep a run from scoring.

The bases were loaded, and who was at bat again? The lead-off man. Kerby Maxwell.

For an instant Kerby's heart sank into his baseball shoes. But then, just as suddenly, he seemed to hear angel voices singing, telling him all was well.

He was at bat, and *he* hadn't sniffed the stuff, and the way Red was pitching he could strike out without half trying and end the game in a glorious defeat!

Seizing a bat, Kerby hurried to the plate. Out on the mound, Red was walking around kicking dirt and shaking his head sharply. Finally he settled down and got ready to pitch. Kerby cocked his bat, ready to swing at Red's first fire-ball and miss.

Red wound up and threw, and too late Kerby saw the look in his eyes.

Red had snapped out of it!

The stuff had worn off! Mrs. Graymalkin had warned them it would not last long, but Kerby had forgotten about that. It was too late to stop his swing, and the ball was floating up like a balloon. . . .

Crack!

Kerby pulled the ball to left field, a high fly straight to the only Wildcat who had not sniffed the stuff — Butterfingers Blatweiler!

When Kerby started running to first, he was watching and praying. "Please! Just once let Butterfingers catch one!"

But of course he didn't. The ball bounced off his glove and he and Buzzy Dugan went chasing after it while the runners tore around the bases and Kerby thought, If I score that's four runs and we win! I've got to not score!

Halfway between first and second Kerby appeared to get his feet tangled. He stumbled and fell. When he got up he seemed to be in great pain. He limped on, barely about to trot.

"Come on, Kerby, run!" yelled the Panthers.

"Hurry! Throw it in, Buzzy!" yelled the Wildcats.

Glancing sideways as he limped along between second and third, Kerby saw Buzzy make a sensational throw to Bruce Carmichael, who had run out into shallow left field. Kerby rounded third with his hopes high again. One more stumble before he reached home and Bruce's throw to the plate would surely beat him. All the other runners had already crossed the plate. The score was tied. Everything depended now on Kerby.

Never had a base runner appeared to be in worse pain. Kerby waited till he was nearly home, and fell down again. Clyde Marshall was planted over the plate with his mitt up, waiting for the throw. Red Blake was on the base line behind Kerby yelling, "Drop it!" Trying to look very game, Kerby pushed himself up on his hands — and at that instant, just as he was getting up, Red Blake backed into him hard, on purpose, and sent him sprawling forward again.

Kerby skidded forward in a cloud of dust. He heard the plop of the ball in Clyde's mitt and felt a hard tag in the middle of his back. It felt wonderful!

The dust cleared enough for him to see his hands, flung out in front of him.

His right hand was on home plate.

"Safe!" yelled Mr. Caldwell. "The Panthers win it, thirteen to twelve!"

Kerby wished he could dig a hole in the ground and stay there, buried forever at home plate. The Panthers would never forgive him. He had spoiled everything. His world was in ruins.

The big finish of the game seemed to have brought everybody to his senses. The Panthers were standing around in a stunned silence. The Wildcats were beginning to look at each other and trying not to grin.

"Well, I guess that settles it," Kerby heard Mr. Carmody growl to Mr. Fowler. "The Panthers are your team."

Crawling to his feet, Kerby stared at Mr. Fowler.

98

EVANSTON PUBLIC LIBRARY
CHILDREN'S DEPARTMENT
1703 ORRINGTON AVENUE
EVANSTON, ILLINOIS 60201

Mr. Fowler's cigar was still in the middle of his face, but the smile was missing. As for the cigar, it had come apart altogether. It looked as if it had exploded under his nose. He threw it away and coughed. His eyes had a glassy look.

"Are you kidding, Uncle Al?" he replied. "I never saw kids play like that before in my whole life. Why, if they played the Tomboys they'd massacre them! They'd humiliate them — and do you know what it's like to have a whole girls' baseball team hopping mad all at once?" He shuddered like a man who knew. "No, sir, these kids are too good! The deal's off! We'll use that team we saw playing over in that park this morning — what's their name? — the Cougars? . . ."

Mr. Fowler and Mr. Carmody were gone, and Mr. Caldwell had hurried off home to go back to work on his trim. The two teams were alone.

"The Cougars! Wow! Let's get there early tomorrow and get good seats!" cried Red Blake.

"I wouldn't miss it!" said Bumps. He scowled at Red, but he could not help grinning at the same time. "You dirty rat, you nearly fixed us good!"

Red grinned back at him sourly.

"Well, if it had been the other way around, you'd have done the same thing!"

100

Bumps guffawed.

"Well . . ." he said, refusing to admit anything. "Hey, whatcha say we play a couple more innings just for fun?"

"You're on!"

Five minutes later the Wildcats were up, and there was a close play at first. All the Wildcats yelled "Safe!" and all the Panthers jumped up and down and yelled, "Aw, he was out a mile!"

Things were back to normal.